Puffin Books

Milly-Molly-Mandy Again

Milly-Molly-Mandy and her Mother and Father, Uncle and Aunty, Grandpa and Grandma are just as busy as ever in this book, in their nice white thatched cottage in the country.

Milly-Molly-Mandy makes several new friends, a new little girl at her school called Bunchy, a tinker family who are living in an old railway coach, and a lonely duck (or, rather, drake) called Dum-dum. She has some special excitements too, like choosing the material for a new dress, being a bridesmaid at a friend's wedding, and waking one morning to find the world full of snow.

This kind, helpful, little country girl has been a book-friend to countless children for nearly fifty years, and doubtless will be for many years to come. Three earlier books about her are also published in Puffins: *Milly-Molly-Mandy Stories*, *More of Milly-Molly-Mandy*, and *Further Doings of Milly-Molly-Mandy*.

For readers of five and over.

Milly-Molly-Mandy Again

Told and drawn by
Joyce Lankester Brisley

Puffin Books

Puffin Books, Penguin Books Ltd, Harmondsworth, Middlesex, England
Penguin Books, 40 West 23rd Street, New York, New York 10010, U.S.A.
Penguin Books Australia Ltd, Ringwood, Victoria, Australia
Penguin Books Canada Ltd, 2801 John Street, Markham, Ontario, Canada L3R 1B4
Penguin Books (N.Z.) Ltd, 182–190 Wairau Road, Auckland 10, New Zealand

First published by George G. Harrap 1948
Published in Puffin Books 1974
Reprinted 1974, 1975, 1977 (twice), 1978, 1979, 1980, 1981, 1982, 1983

Made and printed in Great Britain by
Richard Clay (The Chaucer Press) Ltd, Bungay, Suffolk
Set in Monotype Baskerville

Contents

The Brook

The Nice White Cottage with the Thatched Roof. (where Milly-Molly-Mandy lives)

(near where M·M·M saw the train)

The Barn

The Moggs' Cottage (where little-friend Susan lives)

The Church (where the Black-Smith was married)

Short cut

Dum-dum's enclosure

To the Next Village

MAP of t

Joyce L. Brisley

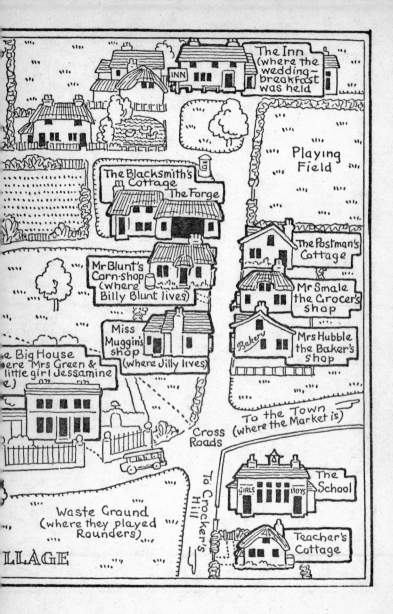

1. Milly-Molly-Mandy has a New Dress

Once upon a time Milly-Molly-Mandy was playing hide-and-seek with Toby the dog.

First Milly-Molly-Mandy threw a stone as far as she could, and then while Toby the dog was fetching it Milly-Molly-Mandy ran the other way and hid in among the gooseberry and currant bushes or behind the wall. And then Toby the dog came to look for her. He was so clever he always found her almost at once – even when she hid in the stable where Twinkletoes the pony lived (only he was out in the meadow eating grass now).

She shut the lower half of the stable door and kept quite quiet, but Toby the dog barked and scratched outside, and wouldn't go away till Milly-Molly-Mandy pushed open the door and came out.

Then Toby the dog was so pleased to see her, and so pleased with himself for finding her, that he jumped up and down on his hind legs, pawing and scratching at her skirt.

And suddenly – *rrrrrip!* – there was a great big

tear all the way down the front of Milly-Molly-Mandy's pink-and-white striped cotton frock.

'Oh dear, oh dear!' said Milly-Molly-Mandy. 'Oh, Toby, just see what you've done now!'

Then Toby the dog stopped jumping up and down, and he looked very sorry and ashamed of himself. So Milly-Molly-Mandy said, 'All right, then! Poor Toby! You didn't mean to do it. But whatever will Mother say? I'll have to go and show her.'

So Milly-Molly-Mandy, looking very solemn and holding her dress together with both hands, walked back through the barnyard where the cows were milked (only they, too, were out in the meadow eating grass now).

Uncle was throwing big buckets of water over the floor of the cowshed, to wash it. 'Now what have you been up to?' he asked, as Milly-Molly-Mandy, looking very solemn and holding her dress together with both hands, passed by.

'I tore my dress playing with Toby, and I'm going in to show Mother,' said Milly-Molly-Mandy.

'Well, well,' said Uncle, sending another big bucketful of water swashing along over the brick floor. 'Now you'll catch it. Tell Mother to send you out to me if she wants you to get a good spanking. I'll give you a proper one!'

'Mother won't let you spank me!' said Milly-Molly-Mandy (she knew Uncle was only joking). 'But she won't like having to mend such a great big tear, I expect. She mended this dress only a little while ago, and now it's got to be done all over again. Come on, Toby.'

So they went through the gate into the kitchen garden (where Father grew the vegetables) and in by the back door of the nice white cottage with the thatched roof where Father and Mother and Grandpa and Grandma and Uncle and Aunty and, of course, Milly-Molly-Mandy all lived together.

'Now what's the matter with little Millicent Margaret Amanda?' said Grandma, who was shelling peas for dinner, as Milly-Molly-Mandy came in, looking very solemn and holding her dress together with both hands.

'I'm looking for Mother,' said Milly-Molly-Mandy.

'She's in the larder,' said Aunty, who was patching sheets with her machine at the kitchen table. 'What have you been up to?'

But Milly-Molly-Mandy went over to the door of the larder, where Mother was washing the shelves.

'Mother,' said Milly-Molly-Mandy, looking very solemn and holding her dress together with both hands, 'I'm dreadfully sorry, but I was playing hide-and-seek with Toby, and we tore my dress. Badly.'

'Dear, dear, now!' said Grandma.

'Whatever next!' said Aunty.

'Let me have a look,' said Mother. She put down her wash-cloth and came out into the kitchen.

Milly-Molly-Mandy took her hands away and showed her frock, with the great big tear all down the front of it.

Mother looked at it. And then she said:

'Well, Milly-Molly-Mandy! That just about finishes that frock! But I was afraid it couldn't last much longer when I mended it before.'

And Grandma said, 'She had really outgrown it.'

And Aunty said, 'It was very faded.'

And Mother said, 'You will have to have a new one.'

Milly-Molly-Mandy *was* pleased to think that was all they said about it. (So was Toby the dog!)

Mother said, 'You can go out in the garden and tear it all you like now, Milly-Molly-Mandy. But don't you go tearing anything else!'

So Milly-Molly-Mandy and Toby the dog had a fine time tearing her old dress to ribbons, so that

Milly-Molly-Mandy showed her frock with the tear all down the front

she looked as if she had been dancing in a furze bush, Grandpa said. And then Mother sent her upstairs to change into her better frock (which was pink-and-white striped, too).

During dinner Mother said:

'I'm going to take Milly-Molly-Mandy down to the Village this afternoon, to buy her some stuff for a new dress.'

Father said, 'I suppose that means you want some more money.' And he took some out of his trousers' pocket and handed it over to Mother.

Grandma said, 'What about getting her something that isn't pink-and-white striped, just for a change?'

Grandpa said, 'Let's have flowers instead of stripes this time.'

Aunty said, 'Something with daisies on would look nice.'

Uncle said, 'Oh, let's go gay while we are about it, and have magenta roses and yellow sunflowers – eh, Milly-Molly-Mandy?'

But Milly-Molly-Mandy said, 'I don't 'spect Miss Muggins keeps that sort of stuff in her shop, so then I can't have it!'

After dinner Milly-Molly-Mandy helped Mother

15

to wash up the plates and things, and then Mother changed her dress, and they put on their hats, and Mother took her handbag, and they went together down the road with the hedges each side towards the Village.

They passed the Moggs' cottage, where little-friend-Susan lived. Little-friend-Susan was helping her baby sister to make mud pies on the step.

'Hullo, Susan,' said Milly-Molly-Mandy. 'We're going to buy me some different new dress stuff at Miss Muggins' shop, because I tore my other one!'

'Are you? How nice! What colour are you going to have this time?' asked little-friend-Susan.

'We don't know yet, but it will be something quite different,' said Milly-Molly-Mandy.

They passed the Forge, where Mr Rudge the Blacksmith and his new boy were making a big fire over an iron hoop which, when it was red-hot, they were going to fit round a broken cart-wheel to mend it. Milly-Molly-Mandy wanted to stay and watch, but Mother said she hadn't time.

So Milly-Molly-Mandy just called out to Mr Rudge, 'We're going to buy some different-coloured dress stuff, because I tore my other one!'

And Mr Rudge stopped to wipe his hot face on his torn shirt sleeve, and said, 'Well, if they'd buy

16

us different-coloured shirts every time we tear ours, you'd see us going about like a couple of rainbows! Eh, Reginald?'

And the new boy grinned as he piled more brushwood on the fire. (He'd got a tear in his shirt too.)

They passed Mr Blunt's corn-shop, where Billy Blunt was polishing up his new second-hand bicycle, which his father had just given him, on the pavement outside.

Milly-Molly-Mandy and Mother stopped a minute to admire it shininess (which was almost like new). And then Milly-Molly-Mandy said, 'We're going to buy me some different-coloured dress stuff, because I tore my other!'

But Billy Blunt wasn't very interested (he was just testing his front brake).

Then they came to Miss Muggins' shop.

And just as they got up to the door so did two other people, coming from the other way. One was an old lady in a black cloak and bonnet, and one was a little girl in a faded flowered dress, with a ribbon round her hair. Mother pushed open the shop door for the old lady and set the little bell jangling above, and they all went in together, so that the shop seemed quite full of people, with Miss Muggins behind the counter too.

Miss Muggins didn't know quite whom to serve first. She looked towards the old lady, and the old lady looked towards Mother, and Mother said, 'No, you first.'

So then the old lady said, 'I would like to see something for a dress for a little girl, if you please – something light and summery.'

And Mother said, 'That is exactly what I am wanting, too.'

So then Miss Muggins brought out the different stuffs from her shelves for both her customers to choose from together.

Milly-Molly-Mandy looked at the little girl. She thought she had seen her before. Surely it was the new little girl who had lately come to Milly-Molly-Mandy's school. Only she was in the 'baby class', so they hadn't talked together yet.

The little girl looked at Milly-Molly-Mandy. And presently she pulled at the old lady's arm and whispered something, whereupon the old lady turned and smiled at Milly-Molly-Mandy, so Milly-Molly-Mandy smiled back.

Milly-Molly-Mandy whispered up at Mother (looking at the little girl). 'She comes to our school!'

So then Mother smiled at the little girl. And the old lady and Mother began to talk together as they looked at Miss Muggins' stuffs. And Milly-Molly-Mandy and the little girl began to talk too, as they waited.

Milly-Molly-Mandy found out that the little girl was called Bunchy, and the old lady was her grandmother, and they lived together in a little cottage quite a long way from the school and the cross-roads, in the other direction from Milly-Molly-Mandy's.

Bunchy hadn't come to school before because she couldn't walk so far. But now she was bigger, and Granny walked with her half the way and she ran the rest by herself. She liked coming to school, but she had never played with other little girls and boys before, and it all felt very strange and rather frightening. So then Milly-Molly-Mandy said they should look out for each other at school next Monday, and play together during play-time. And she told her about little-friend-Susan, and Billy Blunt, and Miss Muggins' Jilly, and other friends at school.

Then Mother said to Miss Muggins, 'And this is all you have in the way of printed cottons? Well, now, I wonder, Milly-Molly-Mandy –'

And Bunchy's Grandmother said, 'Look here, Bunchy, my dear –'

So they both went up to the counter.

There was a light blue silky stuff which Mother and Bunchy's Grandmother said was 'not serviceable.' And a stuff with scarlet poppies and corn-flowers all over it which they said was 'not suitable'. And there was a green chintz stuff which they said was too thick. And a yellow muslin which they said was too thin. And there was a stuff with little bunches of daisies and forget-me-nots on it. And a big roll of pink-and-white striped cotton. And there was nothing more (except flannelette or bolton-sheeting and that sort of thing, which wouldn't do at all).

Milly-Molly-Mandy thought the one with daisies and forget-me-nots was much the prettiest. So did Bunchy. Milly-Molly-Mandy thought a dress of that would be a very nice change.

But Miss Muggins said, 'I'm afraid I have only this short length left, and I don't know when I shall be having any more in.'

So Mother and Bunchy's Grandmother spread it out, and there was really only just enough to make one little frock. Bunchy's Grandmother turned to look at the pink-and-white striped stuff.

Bunchy said, 'That's Milly-Molly-Mandy's stuff, isn't it? It's just like the dress she has on.'

Milly-Molly-Mandy said, 'Do you always have flowers on your dresses?'

'Yes,' said Bunchy, 'because of my name, you

21

know. I'm Violet Rosemary May, but Granny calls me Bunchy for short.'

Milly-Molly-Mandy said to Mother, 'She ought to have that stuff with the bunches of flowers on, oughtn't she? The striped one wouldn't really suit her so well as me, would it?'

Mother said, 'Well, Milly-Molly-Mandy, we do know this striped stuff suits you all right, and it washes and wears well. I'm afraid that blue silky stuff doesn't look as if it would wash, and the yellow muslin wouldn't wear. So perhaps you'd better have the same again. I'll take two yards of this striped, please, Miss Muggins.'

Milly-Molly-Mandy looked once more at the flowery stuff, and she said, 'It *is* pretty, isn't it!

But if Bunchy comes to school I can see it on her, can't I?'

Bunchy's Grandmother said, 'It would be very nice if you could come and see it on Bunchy at home too! If Mother would bring you to tea one Saturday, if you don't mind rather a walk, you could play in the garden with Bunchy, and I'm sure we should both be very pleased indeed, shouldn't we, Bunchy?'

Bunchy said, 'Yes! We should!'

Mother said, 'Thank you very much. We should like to come' – though she had not much time for going out to tea as a rule, but she was sure Aunty would get tea for them all at home for once.

So it was settled for them to go next Saturday, and the little girl called Bunchy was very pleased indeed about it, and so was Milly-Molly-Mandy.

Then Miss Muggins handed over the counter the two parcels, and Milly-Molly-Mandy and Bunchy each carried her own dress stuff home.

And when Milly-Molly-Mandy opened her parcel to show Father and Grandpa and Grandma and Uncle and Aunty what had been bought for her new dress after all, there was a beautiful shiny red ribbon there too, which Mother had bought to tie round Milly-Molly-Mandy's hair when she wore the new dress. So that would make quite a nice change, anyhow.

And as little-friend-Susan said, if Milly-Molly-Mandy didn't wear her pink-and-white stripes people might not know her at once.

And that would be a pity!

2. Milly-Molly-Mandy Finds a Train

Once upon a time Milly-Molly-Mandy was playing
with Billy Blunt down by the little brook (which,
you know, ran through the fields at the back of the
nice white cottage with the thatched roof where
Milly-Molly-Mandy lived).

They had got their shoes and socks off, and were
paddling about in the water, and poking about
among the stones and moss, and enjoying themselves
very much. Only it was so interesting just about
where their feet were that they might have missed
seeing something else interesting, a little farther off,
if a woodpecker hadn't suddenly started pecking in
an old tree near by, and made Billy Blunt look up.

He didn't see the woodpecker, but he did see the
something else.

'I say – what's that, there?' said Billy Blunt,
standing up and staring.

'What's what, where?' said Milly-Molly-Mandy,
standing up and staring too.

'There,' said Billy Blunt, pointing.

25

And Milly-Molly-Mandy looked there. And she saw, in the meadow on the farther side of the brook, what looked like a railway train. Only there was no railway near the meadow.

'It looks like a train,' said Milly-Molly-Mandy.

'Um-m,' said Billy Blunt.

'But how did it get there?' said Milly-Molly-Mandy.

'Must have been pulled there,' said Billy Blunt.

'But what for? Who put it there? When did it come?' said Milly-Molly-Mandy.

Billy Blunt didn't answer. He splashed back to get his boots and socks, and he splashed across the

They walked all round it, staring hard

brook with them, and sat on the grass on the other side, and began to dab his feet with his handkerchief. So Milly-Molly-Mandy splashed across with her shoes and began to put them on too. And with her toes scrunched up in the shoes (because they were still damp and wouldn't straighten out at first) she ran and hopped after Billy Blunt, up the little bank and across the grass to the train.

They walked all round it, staring hard. It hadn't got an engine, or a guard's van. It was just a railway carriage, and it stood with its big iron wheels in the grass, looking odd and out-of-place among the daisies and buttercups.

'It's like a funny sort of house,' said Milly-Molly-Mandy, climbing up to peep in the windows.

'I wish we could play in it. Look – that could be the kitchen, and that's the sitting-room, and that's the bedroom. I wish we could get in!'

It had several doors either side, each with a big 3 painted on. Billy Blunt tried the handles in turn. They all seemed to be locked. But the last one wasn't! It opened heavily, and they could get into one compartment.

'It's old,' said Billy Blunt, looking about. 'I expect they've thrown it away.'

'What a waste!' said Milly-Molly-Mandy. 'Well,

it's ours now. We found it. We can live in it, and go journeys!'

It was very exciting. They shut the door and they opened the windows. And then they sat down on the two wooden seats, and pretended they were going away for a holiday. When they stood up, or walked to the windows to look out, it was difficult to do it steadily, because the train rushed along so fast! Once it let out a great long whistle, so that Milly-Molly-Mandy jumped; and Billy Blunt grinned and did it again.

'We are just going through a station,' he explained.

The next moment Milly-Molly-Mandy nearly fell over and knocked Billy Blunt.

'We've stopped suddenly – the signal must be up,' she explained. So they each hung out of a window to look. 'Now it's down and we're going on again,' said Milly-Molly-Mandy.

'We're going into a tunnel now,' said Billy Blunt, pulling up his window by the strap. So Milly-Molly-Mandy pulled up hers – to keep the smoke out!

When the train stopped at last they got out, and everything looked quite different all round. They were by the sea, and the train was a house. One of the seats was a table, and they laid Billy Blunt's damp handkerchief on it as a tablecloth, and put a rusty tin filled with buttercups in the middle.

But after a while Billy Blunt began to feel hungry, and then, of course, they knew it must be time to think of going home. So at last they shut the door of their wonderful train-house, and planned to meet there again as early as possible the next day.

And then they jumped back over the brook, and Billy Blunt went one way across the field, to his home by the corn-shop; and Milly-Molly-Mandy went the other way across the field, to the nice white cottage with the thatched roof, where she found Father and Mother and Grandpa and Grandma and Uncle and Aunty just ready to sit down to table.

The next day Milly-Molly-Mandy hurried to get all her jobs done – helping to wash up the breakfast things, and make the beds, and do the dusting. And as soon as she was free to play she ran straight out and down to the brook.

Billy Blunt was just coming across the field from the Village, so she waited for him, and together they crossed over the brook, planning where they would go for their travels today.

'There it is!' said Milly-Molly-Mandy, almost as if she had expected the train to have run away in the night.

And then she stopped. And Billy Blunt stopped too.

There was a man with a cap on, sitting on the roof of the train, fixing up a sort of chimney. And there was a woman with an apron on, sweeping

dust out of one of the doorways. And there was a baby in a shabby old pram near by, squealing. And there was a little dog, guarding a hand-cart piled with boxes and bundles, who barked when he saw Milly-Molly-Mandy and Billy Blunt.

31

'They've got our train!' said Milly-Molly-Mandy, staring.

''Spect it's their train, really,' said Billy Blunt.

Milly-Molly-Mandy edged a little nearer and spoke to the little dog, who got under the cart and barked again (but he wagged his tail at the same time). The woman in the apron looked up and saw them.

Milly-Molly-Mandy said, 'Good morning. Is this your train?'

'Yes, it is,' said the woman, knocking dust out of the broom.

'Are you going to live in it?' asked Milly-Molly-Mandy.

'Yes, we are,' said the woman. 'Bought and paid for it, we did, and got it towed here, and it's going to be our home now.'

'Is this your baby?' asked Billy Blunt, jiggling the pram gently. The baby stopped crying and stared up at him. 'What's it's name?'

The woman smiled then. 'His name is Thomas Thomas, like his father's,' she said, 'So it don't matter whether you call either of 'em by surname or given-name, it's all one.'

Just then the man on the roof dropped his hammer down into the grass, and called out. 'Here, mate, just chuck that up, will you?'

So Billy Blunt threw the hammer up, and the man caught it and went on fixing the chimney, while Billy Blunt watched and handed up other things as they were wanted. And the man told him that this end of the carriage was going to be the kitchen (just as Milly-Molly-Mandy had planned!), and the wall between it and the next compartment was to be taken away so as to make it bigger. The other end was the bedroom, with the long seats for beds.

Milly-Molly-Mandy stayed jiggling the pram to keep the baby quiet, and making friends with the little dog. And the woman told her she had got some stuff for window-curtains in the hand-cart there; and that they planned to make a bit of a garden round, to grow potatoes and cabbages in, so the house would soon look more proper. She said her husband was a tinker, and he hoped to get work mending pots and kettles in the villages near, instead of tramping about the country looking for it, as they had been doing.

She asked Milly-Molly-Mandy if she didn't think the baby would have quite a nice home, after a bit? And Milly-Molly-Mandy said she DID!

Presently the woman brought out from the hand-

33

cart a frying-pan, and a newspaper parcel of
sausages, and a kettle (which Milly-Molly-Mandy
filled for her at the brook). So then Milly-Molly-
Mandy and Billy Blunt knew it was time to be
going.

They said good-bye to the man and woman, and
stroked the little dog. (The baby was asleep.) And

as they were crossing back over the brook the man
called after them:

'If you've got any pots, pans, and kettles to
mend, you know where to come to find Thomas
Tinker!'

So after that Milly-Molly-Mandy and Billy Blunt
were always on the look-out for anyone who had a
saucepan, frying-pan, or kettle which leaked or had
a loose handle, and offered at once to take it to
Thomas Tinker's to be mended. And people were

very pleased, because Thomas Tinker mended small things quicker than Mr Rudge the Blacksmith did, not being so busy making horse-shoes and mending ploughs and big things. Thomas Tinker and his wife were very grateful to Milly-Molly-Mandy and Billy Blunt.

But as Milly-Molly-Mandy said, 'If we can get them plenty of work then they can go on living here. And if we can't have that train for ourselves I like next best for Mr Tinker and Mrs Tinker and Baby Tinker to have it – don't you, Billy?'

And Billy Blunt did.

3. Milly-Molly-Mandy and the Surprise Plant

Once upon a time Milly-Molly-Mandy was busy in her own little garden beside the nice white cottage with the thatched roof, planting radish seeds.

Milly-Molly-Mandy's father grew all sorts of vegetables in his big garden – potatoes and turnips and cabbages and peas, which Father and Mother and Grandpa and Grandma and Uncle and Aunty and Milly-Molly-Mandy ate every day for dinner. And he grew fruit too – gooseberries and raspberries and currants and apples, which Mother made into jams and puddings and pies for them all. But, some-how, nothing ever tasted *quite* so good as the things which grew in Milly-Molly-Mandy's own little garden!

There wasn't much room in it, of course, so she could grow only small things, like radishes, or spring-onions, or lettuces, and mostly there wasn't enough of them to give more than a tiny taste each to such a big family as Milly-Molly-Mandy's. But every one enjoyed those tiny tastes extra specially much, so that they always seemed to be a real feast!

Well this time Milly-Molly-Mandy was planting quite a number of seeds, because she thought it would be nice to have enough radishes to give at least two each to Father and Mother and Grandpa and Grandma and Uncle and Aunty and perhaps to little-friend-Susan and Billy Blunt, and, of course,

Milly-Molly-Mandy her own self. (How many's that?)

She was just crumbling earth finely with her fingers to cover up the seeds, when who should come along the road but Mr Rudge the Blacksmith, looking very clean and tidy. (He was going for a walk with the young lady who helped Mrs Hubble in the Baker's shop.)

37

'Hullo, Mr Rudge,' said Milly-Molly-Mandy, looking up at him over the hedge.

'Hullo, there!' said Mr Rudge, looking down at her over the hedge. 'What's this I see – some one digging the garden with her nose?'

'I don't dig with my nose!' said Milly-Molly-Mandy. 'I'm planting radish seeds, with my hands. But my nose tickled and – I rubbed it. Is it muddy?'

'That's all right,' said the Blacksmith. 'I always notice things grow best for people who get muddy noses. Well, what's it going to be this time?'

'Radishes,' said Milly-Molly-Mandy. 'A lot of them. For Father and Mother and Grandpa and Grandma and Uncle and Aunty. And some over – I hope.'

'Bless my boots!' said the Blacksmith. 'You've got a family to feed, no mistake. You ought to try growing something like – Now, wait a minute! I believe I've got an idea. Supposing I were to give you a plant; have you got any room for it?'

'What sort of a plant?' asked Milly-Molly-Mandy with interest.

'It's some I'm growing myself, and I've got one to spare. I don't believe your Dad's got any, so you'd have it all to yourself.'

'Is it something you can eat?' asked Milly-Molly-Mandy.

'Rather! – puddings, pies, what-not,' said the Blacksmith.

'Enough for Father and Mother and Grandpa and Grandma and Uncle and Aunty?' asked Milly-Molly-Mandy.

'Yes, and you too.'

'Could it go in there?' asked Milly-Molly-Mandy excitedly, pointing to a space beside the radish seeds. 'There's nothing in there yet. How big is the plant?'

'Oh, about *so* big,' said the Blacksmith, holding his hands five or six inches apart. 'It'll want a good rich soil. Got any rotten grass-cuttings?'

'Father has, I think,' said Milly-Molly-Mandy, 'he puts it in a heap over there to rot.'

'Well, you ask him to let you have some, quite a nice lot, and put it on the earth there, and I'll bring you along the plant tomorrow. It's a surprise plant – you stick it in and see what'll happen.'

'Thank you very much, Mr Rudge,' said Milly-Molly-Mandy, wondering whatever it could be.

Mr Rudge the Blacksmith went on down the road with the young lady (who had been patiently waiting all this time), and Milly-Molly-Mandy ran to

39

ask Father if she could have some of the rotten grass-cuttings. He brought her some spadefuls (it was all brown and messy and didn't look the least bit like grass, but he said it was just how plants liked it), and she dug it into the space beside the radish seeds and hoped Mr Rudge wouldn't forget about the Surprise Plant.

And Mr Rudge didn't.

The very next evening, when he'd done banging horse-shoes on his anvil with a great big hammer, he took off his leather apron and shut up his forge; and presently Milly-Molly-Mandy, who was looking out for him, saw him coming along up the road.

He'd got the plant with its roots in a lump of earth wrapped in thick paper in his pocket.

Milly-Molly-Mandy helped him to take it out very carefully. And then he helped Milly-Molly-Mandy to plant it in the space beside the radish seeds.

And there it stood, looking rather important all by itself (because, of course, the radishes weren't up yet).

'It'll want a lot of water, mind,' said the Black-smith, as he went out of the gate back to his supper, which he said was waiting for him. So Milly-Molly-Mandy said yes, good-bye, and thank you, and then she went and told Father about it.

Father came and looked at the plant very care-fully (it had two rough scratchy leaves and two smooth seed-leaves). And Father said, 'A Surprise Plant, is it? Well, well!'

Then Mother came out and she looked at the plant, and she said. 'Isn't it a marrow?'

But Milly-Molly-Mandy was quite sure it wasn't a marrow because Mr Rudge had said that Father hadn't got any like this in his garden, and Father had lots of marrows.

Well, the Surprise Plant soon felt at home, and it began to GROW.

The radishes started to come up, but the Surprise Plant came faster. It spread out branches along the earth, with tendrils which curled round any stalk or twig they met and held fast. Soon it covered all the little radishes with its great green scratchy leaves, and filled up all Milly-Molly-Mandy's little garden.

Then it began to open big yellow flowers here and there, so that Milly-Molly-Mandy called out, 'Oh, come quick and look at my Surprise Flowers!' and Father and Mother and Grandpa and Grandma and Uncle and Aunty came to look.

Father said, 'Well, it seems to be getting on all right!'

And Mother said, 'Surely it's a marrow!'

42

And Grandpa said, 'No, 'tisn't a marrow.'

And Grandma said, 'It's got much the same sort of flower as a marrow.'

And Uncle said, 'You'll soon see what it is!'

And Aunty said, 'Whatever it is, it looks as if Milly-Molly-Mandy will be giving us a good big taste this time!'

But Milly-Molly-Mandy said, 'I don't see what there is to *eat* here – and there won't be any radishes now, because they're all hidden up in leaves.'

After a while Milly-Molly-Mandy noticed that one of the flowers had a sort of round yellow ball below the petals, just where the stalk joins on; and as the flower faded the ball began to grow bigger.

She brought Mother to look at it.

Mother said at once, 'Why! I know what it is now!'

Milly-Molly-Mandy said, '*What?*'

And Mother said, 'Of course! It's a pumpkin!'

'Oh-h-h!' said Milly-Molly-Mandy.

Fancy! – a real pumpkin, like what Cinderella went to the ball in drawn by mice, growing in Milly-Molly-Mandy's own little garden!

'Oh-h!' said Milly-Molly-Mandy again.

She didn't mind now if the radishes were spoiled – but anyhow enough came up to give one little

43

red one each to Father and Mother and Grandpa and Grandma and Uncle and Aunty and a weeny one for Milly-Molly-Mandy herself (and how many's that?) – for just think! soon she would be able to go out into her very own little garden and cut a great big pumpkin for them!

Father and Mother and Grandpa and Grandma and Uncle and Aunty began to say, 'How's your coach getting on, Cinderella?' when they met her; and Uncle pretended he'd just seen a mouse running that way to gallop off with it to the ball!

It was a lovely hot summer, which was just what the pumpkin liked (as well as Milly-Molly-Mandy), and it grew and it grew. And do you know, other little pumpkin balls grew under other flowers too, and two of them grew so big that Father gave Milly-Molly-Mandy some straw to put on the ground underneath, for them to rest on. But the first pumpkin grew biggest.

When Mr Rudge the Blacksmith passed along that way he always stopped to look over the hedge, and he said her pumpkin was bigger than any of his own!

Well, September came, and corn was cut, and apples were picked, and the yearly Harvest Festival was to be held in the Village Church. Grown-ups sent in their gifts the day before, to decorate the Church, but children were to have a special Service in the afternoon, and bring their own offerings then.

Father sent in a big marrow and some of his best pears. Mother sent some pots of jam. Grandpa sent a large bunch of late roses. Grandma sent a little cream-cheese. Uncle sent a basket of nice brown eggs. Aunty sent some bunches of lavender.

And what do you suppose Milly-Molly-Mandy took to the Children's Service?

Well, first she looked at her pumpkins, the great big one and the second-best one. And then she said to Mother, 'Mother, what is a Harvest Festival for? – why do you send fruit and things to Church?'

Mother said, 'It's to say "thank you" to God for giving us such a lot of good things.'

'But what becomes of them, those apples, and the jam?' asked Milly-Molly-Mandy.

'Vicar sends them to the Cottage Hospital generally, so the people there can enjoy them.'

'Does God like that, when they're given to Him?' asked Milly-Molly-Mandy.

'Yes,' said Mother. 'He takes the *giving* part, the being thankful part, and the rest Vicar sends to people who need it most, so it's a double giving.'

'Well, I'm very thankful indeed for lots of things!'

On Sunday afternoon they all walked to Church

said Milly-Molly-Mandy. 'So hadn't I better give my pumpkin? We could eat the second-best one and the other little ones ourselves, couldn't we?'

So on the Sunday afternoon they all walked across the fields to Church, in their best clothes, Father and Mother and Grandpa and Grandma and Uncle and Aunty and Milly-Molly-Mandy – AND the pumpkin. She had cut through its stalk herself with a big knife (Father helping), and cleaned it carefully with a damp cloth (Mother helping), and it was so big and heavy that Father had to carry it for her till they came to the Church.

There was quite a number of children carrying things in: little-friend-Susan had a bunch of flowers from her garden, marigolds and Michaelmas-daisies, and nasturtiums, and Billy Blunt brought a basket of little yellow apples which grew by their back fence.

Milly-Molly-Mandy sat in a pew, next to Mother, looking over the big pumpkin in her lap till the time came to give it up.

And then all the children walked in a line to the front of the Church, and Vicar took their gifts one after another and laid them out on a table.

Milly-Molly-Mandy was so pleased to have such a beautiful pumpkin to give that when she had got rid of the burden she ran hoppity-skip back up the aisle, forgetting she was in Church till she saw Mother's face smiling but making a silent 'Ssh!' to her. And then she slid quietly into her seat, and sat admiring the things decorating the Church – the bunches of corn, and fancy loaves of bread (she guessed Mrs Hubble the Baker had sent those), the baskets of fruit and vegetables and flowers and eggs, and pots of preserves with the sun shining through them.

And the pumpkin lay, smooth and round and yellow, among the other things which the children had brought. (But somehow it didn't look quite so awfully big and important there in Church as it had done at home!)

When the Service was over everybody went home. And at tea-time Mother said, 'This week I ought to make some more jam. I was thinking how very nice it would be if we could have pumpkin-and-ginger jam this year, as a change from marrow-and-ginger!'

Then they all looked hopefully at Milly-Molly-Mandy.

And Milly-Molly-Mandy said at once, 'Yes! it would! Shall I go and cut my second-best pumpkin now? And the other little pumpkins?'

So that week Mother made lots of pots of pumpkin-and-ginger jam, Milly-Molly-Mandy helping. And on Saturday Mother let her ask little-friend-Susan and Billy Blunt to tea, and they all had pumpkin-and-ginger jam on their bread-and-butter (as well as chocolate cake and currant buns).

And Father and Mother and Grandpa and Grandma and Uncle and Aunty and little-friend-Susan and Billy Blunt and her own self all thought it was the very best jam they had ever tasted.

And the next time she saw Mr Rudge the Blacksmith, Milly-Molly-Mandy gave him a little pot of pumpkin jam all to himself, to say thank-you-for-giving-me-the-Surprise-Plant.

4. Millie-Molly-Mandy and the Blacksmith's Wedding

Once upon a time Milly-Molly-Mandy was going to a wedding.

It wasn't just the ordinary sort of wedding, where you stared through the churchyard railings, wondering at ladies walking outdoors in their party clothes and who the man in the tight collar was.

This was a very important wedding indeed.

Mr Rudge the Blacksmith was marrying the young lady who helped in Mrs Hubble the Baker's shop. AND (which Milly-Molly-Mandy thought the most important part) there were to be two bridesmaids. And the bridesmaids were Milly-Molly-Mandy and little-friend-Susan.

Milly-Molly-Mandy was sorry that Billy Blunt couldn't be a bridesmaid too, but Billy Blunt said he didn't care because *he* thought the most important part came later.

In the Village, in olden days, when the blacksmith or any of his family got married, he used to

'fire the anvil' outside his forge, with real gunpowder, to celebrate! That's what Mr Rudge the
Blacksmith said. He said his father had been married
that way, and his uncle, and both his aunts, and his
grandpa, and his great-grandpa a long time back.
And that was how he meant to be married too,
quite properly.

Billy Blunt didn't think many blacksmiths could
be properly married, for he had never seen a blacksmith's wedding before, nor even *heard* one, and
neither had Milly-Molly-Mandy, nor little-friend-
Susan.

Anyhow, though he wasn't a bridesmaid, Billy
Blunt had a proper invitation to the wedding, like
Mr and Mrs Blunt (Billy Blunt's father and mother),
and Mr and Mrs Moggs (little-friend-Susan's father
and mother), and Milly-Molly-Mandy's Father and
Mother and Grandpa and Grandma and Uncle and
Aunty, and some other important friends. (For, of
course, only important friends get proper invitations
to weddings; the other sort have to peep through the
railings or hang round by the lane.)

Well, it was only a few days to the wedding now,
and Milly-Molly-Mandy and little-friend-Susan and
Billy Blunt were coming home from afternoon
school. And when they came to the corn-shop

51

(where Billy Blunt lived) they could hear *clink-clang* noises coming from the Forge near by; so they all went round by the lane to have a look in. (For nobody can pass near a forge when things are going on without wanting to look in.)

Mr Rudge the Blacksmith was mending a plough, which wasn't quite so interesting to watch as shoeing a horse, but there was a nice piece of red-hot metal being hammered and bent to the right shape. The great iron hammer bounced off each time, as if it knew just how hot the metal was and didn't want to stay there long, and the iron anvil rang so loudly at every bang and bounce that the Blacksmith couldn't hear anyone speak. But presently he turned and buried the metal in his fire to heat it again, and the Blacksmith's Boy began working the handle of the bellows up and down till the flames roared and sparks flew.

It was just quiet enough then for Milly-Molly-Mandy to call out:

'Hullo, Mr Rudge.'

And Mr Rudge said, 'Hullo, there! Been turned out of school again, have you? Go on, Reginald, push her up.'

So the boy pushed harder at the handle, and the fire roared and the sparks flew.

'Is that really his name?' asked Milly-Molly-Mandy.

'My name's Tom,' said the boy, pumping away.

'Can't have two Toms here,' said the Blacksmith. 'That's my name. He'll have to be content with Reginald. Now then, out of the way, there!'

They all scattered in a hurry as the Blacksmith brought the piece of metal glowing hot out of the fire with his long-handled tongs, and laid it on the anvil again, and began to drill screw-holes in it. The drill seemed to go through the red-hot iron as easily as if it were cheese. As it cooled off and turned grey and hard again, the Blacksmith put it back into the fire. So then they could talk some more.

'Where do you put the gunpowder when you fire the anvil?' asked Billy Blunt.

'In that hole there,' said the Blacksmith, pointing at his anvil.

So Billy Blunt and Milly-Molly-Mandy and little-friend-Susan bent over to see. And, sure enough, there was a small square hole in the top of the anvil. (You look at an anvil if you get the chance, and see.)

'That won't hold very much,' said little-friend-Susan, quite disappointed.

'It'll hold a famous big bang – you just wait,' said the Blacksmith. 'You don't want me to blow up all the lot of you, do you?'

'Have you got the gunpowder ready?' asked Milly-Molly-Mandy.

'I have,' said Mr Rudge.

'Where do you keep it?' asked little-friend-Susan, looking about.

'Not just around here, I can tell you that much.' said Mr Rudge.

'Where do you get the gunpowder?' asked Billy Blunt.

But the Blacksmith said he wasn't giving away any secrets like that. And he brought the piece of

metal out of the fire and started hammering again.

When he had put it back into the fire Milly-Molly-Mandy said:

'Aunty has nearly finished making our brides-maids' dresses, Mr Rudge.'

'I should hope so!' said the Blacksmith. 'How do you suppose I'm to be married next Saturday if you bridesmaids aren't ready? Go on, Reginald, get a move on.'

'They're long dresses, almost down to our feet,' said little-friend-Susan. 'But we're to have a lot of tucks put in them afterwards, so that we can wear them for Sunday-best. And when we grow the tucks can be let out.'

'That's an idea,' said the Blacksmith. 'I'll ask for tucks to be put in my wedding suit, so that I can wear it for Sunday-best afterwards.'

55

Whereupon the Blacksmith's Boy burst out laughing so loudly, as he worked the bellows, that he made more noise than the other three all put together.

The Blacksmith fished the red-hot metal from the fire, and plunged it for a second into a tank of water near by, and there was a great hissing and steaming, and a lot of queer smell.

'What do you do that for?' asked Billy Blunt.

'Tempers the iron,' said the Blacksmith, trying it against the plough to see if it fitted properly; 'brisks it up, like when you have a cold bath on a hot day.'

He laid it on the anvil, and took up a smaller hammer and began tapping away. So Milly-Molly-Mandy and little-friend-Susan and Billy Blunt thought perhaps it was time to go now, so they said good-bye and went off home to their teas.

And Milly-Molly-Mandy and little-friend-Susan had another trying-on of their bridesmaids' dresses after tea. And Aunty stitched and stitched away, so that they should be ready in time for the wedding.

Well, the great day came. And Milly-Molly-Mandy and little-friend-Susan, dressed alike in long pink dresses with bunches of roses in their hands, followed the young lady who helped Mrs

Hubble the Baker up the aisle of the Church, to where Mr Rudge the Blacksmith was waiting.

Mr Rudge looked so clean in his new navy blue suit with shiny white collar and cuffs and a big white button-hole, that Milly-Molly-Mandy hardly knew him (though she had seen him clean before, when he played cricket on the playing-field, or walked out with the young lady who helped Mrs Hubble the Baker).

Then, when the marrying was done, Milly-Molly-Mandy and little-friend-Susan followed the Bride and Bridegroom down the aisle to the door, while everybody in the pews smiled and smiled, and Miss Bloss, who played the harmonium behind a red curtain, played so loudly and cheerfully, and Reginald the Blacksmith's Boy who pumped the bellows for her (so he did a lot of pumping one way and another) pushed the handle up and down so vigorously, it's a wonder they didn't burst the harmonium between them. (But they didn't often have a wedding to play for.)

Then the two Bridesmaids, with the Bride and Bridegroom, of course, stood outside on the Church step to be photographed.

Then everybody walked in a procession down the lane, past the Blacksmith's house and past the Forge (which was closed), and up the road to the Inn, where a room had been hired for the wedding-breakfast (though it was early afternoon).

And then everybody stood around eating and drinking and making jokes and laughing and making speeches and clapping and laughing a lot more.

And Milly-Molly-Mandy and little-friend-Susan and Billy Blunt ate and laughed and clapped as much as anyone (though I'm not sure if Billy Blunt laughed as much as the others, as he was so busy 'sampling' things).

They had two ice-creams each (as Grandma and one or two others didn't want theirs), and they had a big slice of wedding cake each, as well as helpings of nearly everything else, because Mr Rudge insisted on their having it, though their mothers said they'd had quite enough. (He was a very nice man!)

And THEN came the great moment when everybody came out of the Inn and went to the Forge to fire the anvil.

Mr Rudge unlocked the big doors and fastened them back. And then he and Father and Uncle and Mr Blunt and Mr Smale the Grocer between them pulled and pushed the heavy anvil outside into the

They stood on the Church step to be photographed

lane. (The anvil had been cleaned up specially, so it didn't make their hands as dirty as you might think.)

And then Mr Rudge put some black powder into the little square hole in the anvil (Billy Blunt didn't see where he got it from). And the men-folk arranged a long piece of cord (which they called the fuse) from the hole down on to the ground. And then Mr Rudge took a box of matches from his pocket, and struck one, and set the end of the fuse alight.

And then everybody ran back and made a big half-circle round the front of the Forge and waited.

Mother and Mrs Moggs and Mrs Blunt wanted Milly-Molly-Mandy and little-friend-Susan and Billy Blunt to keep near them, and Mr Rudge kept by the young lady who used to help Mrs Hubble the Baker (but she wasn't going to any more, as she was Mrs Rudge now, and Mr Rudge said she'd have her work cut out looking after him). She seemed very frightened and held her hands over her ears, so he kept his arm round her.

Milly-Molly-Mandy and little-friend-Susan put their hands half over their ears and hopped up and down excitedly. But Billy Blunt put his hands in his pockets and stood quite still. He said he didn't want to waste any of the bang.

The little flame crept along the fuse, nearer and nearer. And it began to creep up the anvil. And they all waited, breathless, for the big bang. They waited. And they waited.

And they waited.

'What's the matter with the thing?' said Mr Rudge, taking his arm away from the young lady who was Mrs Rudge now. 'Has the fuse gone out? Keep back, everybody, it isn't safe yet.'

So they waited some more. But still nothing happened.

At last Mr Rudge walked over to the anvil, and so did the other men (though the women didn't want them to).

'Ha!' said Mr Rudge. 'Fuse went out just as it

61

reached the edge of the anvil. Now what'll we do? It's too short to re-light.'

'I've got some string,' said Billy Blunt, and he rummaged in his breeches pocket.

'Bring it here, and let's have a look at it,' said Mr Rudge.

So Billy Blunt went close and gave it to him (and took a good look into the hole at the same time).

'Will that carry the flame, d'you think?' said Father.

'Might do, if you give it a rub with a bit of candle-wax,' said Mr Smale the Grocer.

'I think I've got a bit of wax,' said Billy Blunt, rummaging in his pocket again.

'Hand it over,' said Mr Rudge. 'What else have you got in there – a general store?'

'It's bees-wax, not candle-wax, though,' said Billy Blunt.

'Never mind, so long as it's wax,' said Mr Blunt.

'It's got a bit stuck,' said Billy Blunt, still rummaging.

'You boys – whatever will you put in your pockets next?' said Mrs Blunt.

'Better turn it inside out,' said Uncle.

So Billy Blunt pulled his whole pocket outside. And there *was* a lot of things in it – marbles, and horse-chestnuts, and putty, and a pocket-knife, and a pencil-holder, and a broken key, and a ha'penny, and several bus tickets, and some other things. And stuck half into the lining at the seam was a lump of bees-wax, which they dug off with the pocket-knife.

'You have your uses, William,' said Mr Rudge. And he waxed the string, and arranged it to hang from the anvil along the ground. And he struck a match and lit the end. And everybody ran back again in a hurry, and made a big half-circle round the anvil, and waited as before.

And the little flame crept along, and it paused and looked as if it were going out, and it crept on again, and it reached the anvil, and it began to creep up, and everybody waited, and Milly-Molly-Mandy and little-friend-Susan put their hands over their ears and smiled at each other, and Billy Blunt put his hands deep in his pockets and frowned straight ahead.

And the little flame crept up the string to the top of the anvil, and everybody held their breath, and Milly-Molly-Mandy pressed her hands hard over her ears, and then she was afraid she might not hear enough so she lifted them off – and, just at that very moment, there came a great big enormous
BANG!

And Milly-Molly-Mandy and little-friend-Susan jumped and gave a shriek because they were so splendidly startled (even though they were expecting it). And Billy Blunt grinned and looked pleased. And everybody began to talk and exclaim together as they went forward to look at the anvil (which

wasn't hurt at all, only a bit dirty-looking round the hole).

Then everybody shook hands with the Blacksmith and his Bride, and told them they certainly had been properly married, and wished them well. And the Blacksmith thanked them all heartily.

And when it came time for Milly-Molly-Mandy

and little-friend-Susan and Billy Blunt to shake hands and say thank-you-for-a-nice-wedding-party, Mr Rudge said:

'Well, now, what sort of a wedding it would have been without you bridesmaids, and Billy Blunt to provide all our requirements out of his ample pockets, I just cannot conceive!'

And everybody laughed, and Mr Rudge smacked Billy Blunt on the shoulder so that he nearly fell over (but it didn't hurt him).

So then Milly-Molly-Mandy and little-friend-Susan and Billy Blunt each knew that they had been very important indeed in helping to give Mr Rudge a really proper Blacksmith's Wedding!

5. Milly-Molly-Mandy and Dum-dum

Once upon a time Milly-Molly-Mandy was wandering past the Big House down by the cross-roads, where the little girl Jessamine, and her mother, Mrs Green, lived (only they were away just now).

There was always a lot of flowers in the garden of the Big House, so it was nice to peep through the gate when you passed. Besides, Mr Moggs, little-friend-Susan's father, worked there (he was the gardener), and Milly-Molly-Mandy could see him now, weeding with a long-handled hoe.

'Hello, Mr Moggs,' Milly-Molly-Mandy called through the gate (softly, because you don't like to shout in other people's gardens, even when you know the people are away). 'Could I come in, do you think?')

Mr Moggs looked up and said, 'Well, now, I shouldn't wonder but what you could!'

So Milly-Molly-Mandy pushed open the big iron gate and slipped through.

'Isn't it pretty here!' she said, looking about her.

'What do you weed it for, when there's nobody to see?'

'Ah,' said Mr Moggs, 'you learn it doesn't do to let things go, in a garden, or anywhere else. Weeds and all suchlike, they get to thinking they own the place if you let 'em alone awhile.'

He went on scratching out weeds, so Milly-Molly-Mandy gathered them into his big wheelbarrow for him.

Presently Mr Moggs scratched out a worm along with a tuft of dandelion, and Milly-Molly-Mandy squeaked because she nearly took hold of it without noticing (only she just didn't).

'Don't you like worms?' asked Mr Moggs.

'No,' said Milly-Molly-Mandy; 'I don't!'

'Ah,' said Mr Moggs. 'I know some one who does, though.'

'Who?' asked Milly-Molly-Mandy, sitting back on her heels.

'Old Dum-dum's very partial to a nice fat worm,' said Mr Moggs. 'Haven't you met old Dum-dum?'

'No,' said Milly-Molly-Mandy. 'Who's old Dum-dum?'

'You come and see,' said Mr Moggs. 'I've got to feed him before I go off home.'

He trundled the barrow to the back garden and emptied it on the rubbish heap, and Milly-Molly-Mandy followed, carrying the worm on a trowel.

Mr Moggs got a little tin full of grain from the tool-shed, and pulled a lettuce from the vegetable bed, and then he went to the end of the garden, Milly-Molly-Mandy following.

There was a little square of grass fenced off with wire-netting in which was a little wooden gate. And in the middle of the square of grass was a little round pond. And standing at the edge of the little round pond, looking very solemn, hunched up in his feathers, was Dum-dum.

'Oh!' said Milly-Molly-Mandy. 'Dum-dum is a duck!'

'Well, he's a drake, really,' said Mr Moggs; 'see the little curly feathers on his tail? That shows he's a gentleman. Lady ducks don't have curls on their tails.' He leaned over the netting and emptied the grain into a feeding-pan lying on the grass. 'Come on, quack-quack!' said Mr Moggs. 'Here's your supper.'

Dum-dum looked round at him, and at Milly-Molly-Mandy. Then he waddled slowly over on his yellow webbed feet, and shuffled his beak in the

pan for a moment. Then he waddled slowly back to his pond, dipped down and took a sip, and stood as before, looking very solemn, hunched up in his feathers, with a drop of water hanging from his flat yellow beak.

'He doesn't want any supper!' said Milly-Molly-Mandy. 'Why doesn't he?'

'Feels lonely, that's what. Misses the folk up at the Big House. They used to come and talk to him sometimes and give him bits. He's the little girl Jessamine's pet.'

'Poor Dum-dum!' said Milly-Molly-Mandy. 'He does look miserable. Would you like a worm, Dum-dum?'

He came waddling over again, and stretched up his beak. And down went the worm, *snip-snap*.

'Doesn't he make a funny husky noise? Has he lost his quack?' asked Milly-Molly-Mandy.

'No,' said Mr Moggs, 'gentlemen ducks never talk so loud as lady ducks.'

'*Huh! huh! huh!*' quacked Dum-dum, asking for more worms as loudly as he could.

So Milly-Molly-Mandy dug with the trowel and found another, a little one, and threw it over the netting.

'Do you suppose worms mind very much?' she asked, watching Dum-dum gobbling.

'Well, I don't suppose they think a great deal about it, one way or t'other,' said Mr Moggs.

He dug over a bit of ground with his spade, and Milly-Molly-Mandy found eight more worms. So Dum-dum made quite a good supper after all.

Then Milly-Molly-Mandy leaned over the wire-netting and tried stroking the shiny green feathers on Dum-dum's head and neck. And though he edged away a bit at first, after a few tries he stood quite still, holding his head down while she stroked as if he rather liked it.

And then suddenly he turned and pushed his beak into Milly-Molly-Mandy's warm hand and left it there, so that she was holding his beak as if she were shaking hands with it! It startled her at first, it felt so funny and cold.

'Ah, he likes you,' said Mr Moggs, wiping his spade with a bunch of grass. 'He's a funny old bird; some he likes and some he doesn't. Well, we must be going.'

'Mr Moggs,' begged Milly-Molly-Mandy, still holding Dum-dum's beak gently in her hand, 'don't you think I might come in sometimes to cheer him up, while his people are away? He's so lonely!'

'Well,' said Mr Moggs, 'I don't see why not – if you don't go bringing your little playmates running around in here too. Look, if I'm not about you can get in by the side gate there.' And he showed her how to unfasten it and lock it up again. 'But mind, I'm trusting you,' said Mr Moggs.

So Milly-Molly-Mandy promised to be very careful indeed.

After that she went into the Big House garden every day after school, to cheer up poor Dum-dum. And he got so cheerful he would run to his fence to meet her, saying, '*Huh! huh! huh!*' directly he heard her coming. She used to go into his enclosure to

play with him, and pour water on to the earth for him to make mud with. (He loved mud!)

One day Milly-Molly-Mandy thought it would be nice if Dum-dum could have a change from that narrow run, so she asked Mr Moggs if she might let him out for a little walk. And Mr Moggs said she might try it, if she watched that he didn't eat the flowers and vegetables or get out into the road. So Milly-Molly-Mandy opened his little wooden gate, and Dum-dum stepped out on his yellow feet, looking at everything with great interest.

He was so good and obedient, he followed her along the garden paths and came where she called, like a little dog. So she often let him out after that. She turned over stones and things for him to hunt slugs and woodlice underneath. Sometimes she took him in the front garden too, and showed him to Billy Blunt through the gate.

One morning Milly-Molly-Mandy was very early for school, because the clock at home was fast. At first, when she found no one round the school gate, she thought it was late; but when she found it wasn't she knew why little-friend-Susan hadn't been ready when she passed the Moggs' cottage!

So, as there was plenty of time, she thought she'd go and visit Dum-dum before school today. So she slipped in by the side gate, and found him busily tidying his feathers in the morning sunshine. He looked surprised and very pleased to see her, and they had a run round the garden and found one slug and five woodlice (which Dum-dum thought

very tasty for breakfast!). Then she shut him back
in his enclosure, and latched his little gate, and shut
the side gate and fastened it as Mr Moggs had
showed her, and went off to school (And she only
just wasn't late, this time!)

Well, they'd sung the hymn, and Miss Edwards
had called their names, and everybody was there
except Billy Blunt and the new little girl called
Bunchy. And they had just settled down for an
arithmetic lesson when the little girl Bunchy hurried
in, looking rather frightened. And she told Miss
Edwards there was a great big goose outside, and
she dared not come in before because she thought
it might bite her!

'A goose!' said Miss Edwards. 'Nonsense! There
are no geese round here.'

And Milly-Molly-Mandy looked up from her
exercise book quickly. But she knew she had shut
Dum-dum up carefully, so she went on again
dividing by seven (which wasn't easy).

And then the door opened again, and Billy Blunt
came in with a wide grin on his face and a note in
his hand. (It was from his mother to ask Miss
Edwards to excuse his being late, because he'd had
to run an errand for his father, who had no one else
to send.)

74

And who DO you think came in with him, pushing between Billy Blunt's legs through the doorway, right into the schoolroom?

It was Dum-dum!

'Billy Blunt!' said Miss Edwards. 'What is this?'

'I couldn't help it, ma'am,' said Billy Blunt. 'He would come in. I tried to shoo him off.' (But I don't really think he had tried awfully hard!)

'You mustn't let it come in here,' said Miss Edwards. 'Turn it out. Sit down, children, and be quiet.' (Because they were all out of their places, watching and laughing at the duck that came to school.)

'Oh, please, Teacher –' said Milly-Molly-Mandy, putting up her hand.

'Sit down, Milly-Molly-Mandy,' said Miss Edwards. 'Take that duck outside, Billy Blunt. Quickly, now.'

But when Billy Blunt tried again to shoo him out Dum-dum slipped away from him, farther in, under the nearest desk. And Miss Muggins' Jilly squealed loudly, and pulled her legs up on to her seat.

'Please, Teacher –' said Milly-Molly-Mandy again. 'Oh, please, Teacher – he's my duck – I mean, he's a friend of mine –'

Who DO you think came in with him?

'What is all this?' said Miss Edwards. 'Be quiet, all of you! Now, Milly-Molly-Mandy – explain.'

So Milly-Molly-Mandy explained who Dum-dum was, and where he lived, and that she thought he had come to look for her – though how he had got out and found his way here she couldn't think. 'Please, Teacher, can I take him back home?' she asked.

'I can't let you go in the middle of school,' said Miss Edwards. 'You can shut him out in the yard now, and take him back after school.'

So Milly-Molly-Mandy walked to the door, saying, 'Come, Dum-dum!'

And Dum-dum ran waddling on his flapping yellow feet after her, all across the floor, saying '*Huh! huh! huh!*' as he went.

How the children did laugh!

Billy Blunt said, 'I'll just see that the gate's shut.' And he hurried outside too (lest Miss Edwards should say he needn't!)

He tried to stroke Dum-dum as Milly-Molly-Mandy did, but Dum-dum didn't know Billy Blunt well enough. He opened his beak wide and said, '*Huhhh!*' at him. So Billy Blunt left off trying and went and shut the gate.

'He must have some water,' said Milly-Molly-

77

Mandy (because she knew ducks are never happy if they haven't).

So they looked about for something to hold water, other than the drinking-mug. And Billy Blunt brought the lid of the dustbox, and they filled it at

the drinking-tap and set it on the ground. And Dum-dum at once began taking sip after sip, as if he had never tasted such nice water before.

So Milly-Molly-Mandy and Billy Blunt left him there, and hurried back to their lessons.

Directly school was over the children rushed out to see Milly-Molly-Mandy lead the duck (drake, I mean) along the road back to his home. (It wasn't

easy with so many people helping!) Mr Moggs was
just coming away from the Big House, but he went
back with her to find out how Dum-dum had
escaped, for his gate was shut as Milly-Molly-
Mandy had left it. And they found Dum-dum had

made a little hole in his wire-netting and pushed
through that way and under the front gate. So Mr
Moggs fastened up the hole.

And while he was doing it Milly-Molly-Mandy
noticed that the windows were open in the Big
House, and the curtains were drawn back.

'Oh!' said Milly-Molly-Mandy. 'Have the
people come back?'

'They're coming tomorrow,' said Mr Moggs. 'Mrs Moggs is just airing the place for them.'

'Then I shan't be able to come and see Dum-dum any more!' said Milly-Molly-Mandy.

And she felt quite sad for some days after that, to think that Dum-dum wouldn't want her any more, though she was glad he wasn't lonely.

Then one day (what DO you think?) Milly-Molly-Mandy met the little girl Jessamine and her mother in the post-office, and the little girl Jessamine's mother said, 'Mr Moggs tells me you used to come and cheer up our old duck while we were away!'

Milly-Molly-Mandy wondered if Mrs Green was cross about it. But she wasn't a bit. She said, 'Jessamine is going to boarding school soon – did you know? – and she was wondering what to do about Dum-dum. Would you like to have him for keeps, when she has gone?'

And the little girl Jessamine said, 'We want him to go to someone who'll be kind to him.'

Milly-Molly-Mandy *was* pleased!

She ran home to give Father the stamps she had been sent to buy, and to ask the family if she might have Dum-dum for keeps.

And Mother said, 'How kind of the Greens!'

And Father said, 'He can live out in the meadow.'

And Grandma said, 'It will be very lonely for him.'

And Grandpa said, 'We must find him a companion.'

And Aunty said, 'You'll have to save up and buy another one.'

And Uncle said, 'I've been thinking of keeping a few ducks myself, down by the brook. Your Dum-dum can live along with them, if you like, Milly-Molly-Mandy.'

Milly-Molly-Mandy was very pleased indeed.

The next day she hurried down to the Big House to tell the little girl Jessamine and her mother. And they let her take Dum-dum home with her at once.

So she led him slowly by the short cut across the fields to the nice white cottage with the thatched roof. And he followed her beautifully all the way. In fact, he walked right over the step and into the kitchen with her!

When Uncle saw him following her about he said:

> 'Milly-Molly had a duck.
>
> It's little head was green.
>
> And everywhere that Milly went
>
> That duck was to be seen!'

'Yes, and he did follow me to school one day, like Mary's little lamb!' said Milly-Molly-Mandy.

And do you know, old Dum-dum didn't want to live down by the brook with the other ducks; it was too far from Milly-Molly-Mandy. He chose to live in the barn-yard with the cows and Twinkle-toes the pony, and drink out of Toby the dog's drinking-bowl. And whenever the garden gate was undone Dum-dum would waddle straight through and make for the back door and knock on it with his beak, till Milly-Molly-Mandy came out to play with him!

6. Milly-Molly-Mandy and the Gang

Once upon a time Milly-Molly-Mandy was in Mr Smale the Grocer's shop, to get some things for Mother. There was someone else just being served, so while she waited she looked from the doorway at Billy Blunt, who was spinning a wooden top on the pavement opposite, outside his father's corn-shop.

Presently some boys came along the road. As they passed Billy Blunt one of the boys kicked his top into the gutter, and another pulled his cap off and threw it on the ground; and then they went on down the road, laughing and shouting to one another.

Billy Blunt looked annoyed. But he only picked up his cap and dusted it and put it on again, and picked up his top and wiped it and went on spinning.

And just then Mr Smale the Grocer said, 'Well, young lady, and what can I do for you this morning?' So Milly-Molly-Mandy had to come away from the door and be served.

Milly-Molly-Mandy had seen the boys before.

They didn't belong to the Village, but had come to stay near by, and they were always about, and always seemed to be making a lot of noise.

Well, Milly-Molly-Mandy got the things Mother wanted – a tin of cocoa, and a tin of mustard, and some root-ginger (for making rhubarb-and-ginger jam). And then she left the shop, to go across and speak to Billy Blunt.

But as she stepped over the step the boys were

coming back again, up her side of the road this time, and they bumped into her so that the basket of groceries was knocked out of her hand. The tins came clattering out, and the paper of root-ginger burst all over the pavement.

84

And instead of saying 'Sorry!' the boys only grinned broadly and went on their way, turning back to look at her now and then.

Billy Blunt came across the road to help.

'Billy!' said Milly-Molly-Mandy, 'I believe they meant to do that! They bumped into me on purpose!'

Billy Blunt said, 'Lot of donkeys.' And began picking up bits of ginger.

'What did they want to do it for?' said Milly-Molly-Mandy. 'And pull your cap off too!'

Billy Blunt only grunted, and picked up more bits of ginger.

Mr Smale the Grocer came to his door to see what was going on, and said, 'Them stupid young things knocked your basket, did they? Tell your mother to give that ginger a rinse in cold water and it'll be all right. Out to make nuisances of themselves, they are. They've got something to learn, stupid young things!'

Miss Muggin's niece, Jilly, came running over. She had been watching from Miss Muggins' Draper's shop opposite.

'They're a gang, they are,' she told Milly-Molly-Mandy and Billy Blunt. 'They try to knock people's

85

hats off and make them drop things all the time. They've got a leader, and they're a gang!'

'They're donkeys,' said Billy Blunt. And he went back to his own side of the pavement, winding up his top as he went.

Milly-Molly-Mandy said, 'Thank you!' to him, and started off home with her basket. And Miss Muggins' Jilly went with her a little way, talking about 'the gang' and the naughty things they did.

'They're silly,' said Milly-Molly-Mandy. 'I shouldn't take any notice of them.'

'Oh, I don't,' said Miss Muggins' Jilly. And she went right on talking about them till they came to the duck-pond. There they parted, and Milly-Molly-Mandy went on up the road to the nice white cottage with the thatched roof, where Mother was waiting for her groceries. (She washed the ginger, and it was all right.)

The next morning little-friend-Susan came round to see if Milly-Molly-Mandy was coming out to play.

Milly-Molly-Mandy was just helping Mother to clean the big preserving-pan that the rhubarb-and-ginger jam had been cooked in. So Mother gave little-friend-Susan a spoon so that she could help to clean it too! And when the pan was as clean as they could make it with their two spoons they washed their sticky hands and faces, and then Mother gave them a big slice of bread-and-jam each to take out into the fields to eat.

So they went over the road and climbed the stile and strolled along the field-path, eating and talking and enjoying themselves very much.

And they were just turning down the lane leading to the Forge (which is always a nice way to go if you're not going anywhere special) when little-friend-Susan said, 'Look at those boys; what are they doing?'

Milly-Molly-Mandy looked, licking jam off her fingers, and she saw they were the boys whom Miss Muggins' Jilly called 'the gang'. They were peeping round the hedge by the next stile.

87

'They're waiting to knock our hats off, only we haven't got any on!' said Milly-Molly-Mandy.

'Hadn't we better go back?' said little-friend-Susan.

'No!' said Milly-Molly-Mandy. 'They're just silly, that's what they are. I'm going on.'

So they went on, and climbed over the stile, Milly-Molly-Mandy first, and then little-friend-Susan.

And just as she had got over one of the boys jumped out of the hedge and knocked the piece of bread-and-jam (only a very small piece now) out of little-friend-Susan's hand into the dirt, and ran behind the hedge again.

Little-friend-Susan didn't like having her last piece of bread-and-jam spoiled. But Milly-Molly-Mandy even more didn't like seeing who the boy was who did it.

'It's Timmy Biggs,' she said – 'you know, that boy who won the race at the Fête, and Billy Blunt used to practise with. Why did he want to do that?'

Little-friend-Susan was looking at her bread-and-jam. 'I can't eat this now,' she said. 'I'll take it to the ducks.' (Because, of course, you never waste bread.)

So Milly-Molly-Mandy just called out, 'You're silly, Timmy Biggs!' at the hedge, and they went on past the Forge and down to the duck-pond. (The Blacksmith wasn't hammering or doing anything interesting, so they didn't stop to watch.)

Billy Blunt was in his garden by the corn-shop, busy with the lock of the old cycle-shed which stood in one corner. He saw them coming down the back lane, and as they didn't pass the garden fence he knew they must have turned the other way. So presently he wandered out and found them by the duck-pond.

There were five ducks quacking and paddling in the water, and little-friend-Susan was tearing her bread into as many bits as she could, but it didn't go very far!

'Hullo, Billy,' said Milly-Molly-Mandy, as soon as he came near. 'What do you think – Timmy Biggs has gone and joined that gang. He knocked Susan's bread-and-jam into the dirt.'

'I saw him with them,' said Billy Blunt.

'We ought to do something,' said Milly-Molly-Mandy.

'Umm,' said Billy Blunt.

'Knock their caps off and see how they like it!' said little-friend-Susan.

'I don't see why we have to be silly just because they are,' said Milly-Molly-Mandy. 'I don't want to be in their sort of gang.'

'Might start a gang of our own,' said Billy Blunt.

'Oh, *yes*!' said Milly-Molly-Mandy and little-friend-Susan exactly together. (So then they had to hold each other's little finger and think of a poet's name before they did anything else. 'Robert Burns!' said Milly-Molly-Mandy. 'Shakespeare!' said little-friend-Susan.)

Then they set to work to think what they could do in their gang.

'It must be quite different from that other one,' said Milly-Molly-Mandy. 'They knock things down, so we pick things up.'

'And they leave field-gates open, so we close them,' said little-friend-Susan.

'And we could have private meetings in our old cycle-shed,' said Billy Blunt. 'It's got a lock and key.'

That was a splendid idea, and the new gang got busy right away, clearing dust and spiders out of the cycle-shed. (There were no bicycles kept there now.)

And while they were in the middle of it – sweeping the floor with the garden broom, scraping the corners out with the garden trowel, and rubbing the tiny window with handfuls of grass – suddenly they heard shouting and footsteps running. And through the fence they saw boys tearing down the road from Mrs Jakes the Postman's wife's gate.

'Come on,' said Billy Blunt to his gang.

And they all ran out to see what had happened.

Mrs Jakes was in her yard, flapping her hands with annoyance, her clean washing lying all along the ground.

'Oh-h-h!' she cried, 'those boys! They untied the end of my clothes-line. And now look at it!'

Billy Blunt picked up the end of the rope, and they all tried to lift the clothes-line to tie it up again, but it was too heavy with all the washing on it. So Mrs Jakes told them to un-peg the clothes and take them carefully off the ground, so as not to dirty them any more. The grass was clean and the things were nearly dry, so they weren't much hurt – only one or two tea-cloths needed to be rinsed where they had touched against the fence.

The new gang collected the pegs into a basket,

They all ran out to see what had happened

and helped Mrs Jakes to carry the washing into her kitchen, and she was very grateful for their help.

'It's not near so bad as I thought when I first saw that line come down,' she said. 'Do you three like gooseberries?'

She gave them a handful each, and they went back to the cycle-shed and held a private meeting at once.

The next day Miss Muggins' Jilly found out about

94

the new gang, and asked if she could join. She
wanted to so much that they let her. And they
made up some rules, such as not telling secrets of
their private meetings, or where the key of the
cycle-shed was hidden, and about being always on
the look-out to pick things up, and mend things,
and shut gates, and about being faithful to the rules
of the gang, and that sort of thing.

Well, they were kept quite busy in one way and
another. They helped Mrs Critch the Thatcher's
wife to collect her chickens when they were all let
loose into the road. And they kept an eye on the
field-gates, that cows and sheep didn't get a chance
of straying. And they rescued hats and caps and
things belonging to other children when they were
knocked off unexpectedly. And whenever there was
anything important to discuss or if any of their gang
had anything given to them, such as apples, they
would go along to the cycle-shed and call a private
meeting.

They liked those meetings!

One day, when they had been having a meeting,
they saw Timmy Biggs hanging about by the Blunt's
fence, alone. And when Billy Blunt purposely
wandered over that way Timmy Biggs said to him,
'I say – I suppose you wouldn't let me join your

gang? I don't like that other one – I'd rather join yours. Could I?'

Billy Blunt told him he'd have to think about it and ask the others.

So he did, and they agreed to let Timmy Biggs join, if he promised to keep the rules. So he joined, and they started a rounders team on the waste ground near the school.

Then two of the other boys took to hanging round watching, as if they wanted to join in. And presently they spoke to Billy Blunt.

'We don't like our gang much; we're tired of it,' they said. 'It was his idea.' And they pointed at the third boy, who was sauntering by himself down the lane. He had been their gang leader.

With seven of them now they could play rounders splendidly, with Billy Blunt's bat, and Milly-Molly-Mandy and Miss Muggins' Jilly taking turns to lend their balls. The cycle-shed was too small now to hold their meetings, so they used it as a place to put the gang belongings in or to write important notices.

Not long after, just as the whole gang was going to begin a game, Milly-Molly-Mandy and Billy Blunt and little-friend-Susan began whispering together, and glancing at where the once-leader of the other gang was sitting under a tree, watching them (but pretending not to), because he had nothing much else to do.

When they had finished whispering Billy Blunt walked over to the tree.

'If you want to join in, come on,' he said.

'Well, I don't mind,' said the boy. And he got up quite quickly.

They had a grand game with so many players, and they worked up a very fine team indeed.

And do you know, when, a few weeks later, the time came for those three visiting boys to leave the Village and go back home, nobody felt so very pleased to see them go.

And Milly-Molly-Mandy and Billy Blunt and little-friend-Susan and Miss Muggins' Jilly and Timmy Biggs would have been quite sorry, only that now they could just manage to squeeze into the cycle-shed to have their private meetings again!

7. Milly-Molly-Mandy goes Sledging

Once upon a time, one cold grey wintry day, Milly-Molly-Mandy and the others were coming home from school.

It was such a cold wintry day that everybody turned up their coat-collars and put their hands in their pockets, and such a grey wintry day that it seemed almost dark already, though it was only four o'clock.

'Oooh! isn't it a cold grey wintry day!' said Milly-Molly-Mandy.

'Perhaps it's going to snow,' said little-friend-Susan.

'Hope it does,' said Billy Blunt. 'I'm going to make a sledge.'

Whereupon Milly-Molly-Mandy and little-friend-Susan said both together: 'Ooh! will you give us a ride on it?'

'Haven't made it yet,' said Billy Blunt. 'But I've got an old wooden box I can make it of.'

Then he said good-bye and went in at the side

gate by the corn-shop where he lived. And Milly-Molly-Mandy and little-friend-Susan ran together along the road to the Moggs' cottage, where little-friend-Susan lived. And then Milly-Molly-Mandy went on alone to the nice white cottage with the thatched roof, where Toby the dog came capering out to welcome her home.

It felt so nice and warm in the kitchen, and it smelled so nice and warm too, that Milly-Molly-Mandy was quite glad to be in.

'Here she comes!' said Grandma, putting the well-filled toast-rack on the table.

'There you are!' said Aunty, breaking open hot scones and buttering them on a plate.

'Just in time, Milly-Molly-Mandy!' said Mother, pouring boiling water into the teapot. 'Call the men-folk in to tea, but don't keep the door open long.'

So Milly-Molly-Mandy called, and Father and Grandpa and Uncle soon came in, rubbing their hands, very pleased to get back into the warm again.

'Ah! Nicer indoors than out,' said Grandpa.

'There's a feel of snow in the air,' said Uncle.

'Shouldn't wonder if we had a fall before morning,' said Father.

'Billy Blunt's going to make a sledge, and he *might* let Susan and me have a ride, if it snows,' said Milly-Molly-Mandy. And she wished very much that it would.

That set Father and Uncle talking during tea of the fun they used to have in their young days sledging down Crocker's Hill.

Milly-Molly-Mandy did wish it would snow soon.

The next day was Saturday, and there was no school, which always made it feel different when you woke up in the morning. But all the same Milly-Molly-Mandy thought something about her little bedroom looked different somehow, when she opened her eyes.

Everything outside was white as white could be

'Milly-Molly-Mandy!' called Mother up the stairs, as she did every morning.

'Yoo-oo!' called Milly-Molly-Mandy, to show she was awake.

'Have you looked out of your window yet?' called Mother.

'No, Mother,' called Milly-Molly-Mandy, sitting up in bed. 'Why?'

'You look,' said Mother. 'And hurry up with your dressing.' And she went downstairs to the kitchen to get the breakfast.

So Milly-Molly-Mandy jumped out of bed and looked.

'Oh!' she said, staring. 'Oh-h!'

For everything outside her little low window was white as white could be, except the sky, which was dark, dirty grey and criss-crossed all over with snow-flakes flying down.

'Oh-h-h!' said Milly-Molly-Mandy again.

And then she set to work washing and dressing in a great hurry (and wasn't it cold!) and she rushed downstairs.

She wanted to go out and play at once, almost before she had done breakfast, but Mother said there was plenty of time to clear up all her porridge, for she mustn't go out until the snow stopped falling.

Milly-Molly-Mandy hoped it would be quick and stop. She wanted to see little-friend-Susan, and to find out if Billy Blunt had begun making his sledge.

But Father said, the deeper the snow the better for sledging. So then Milly-Molly-Mandy didn't know whether she most wished it to snow or to stop snowing!

'Well,' said Mother, 'it looks as if it means to go on snowing for some while yet, so I should wish for that if I were you! Suppose you be Jemima-Jane and help me to make the cakes this morning, as you can't go out.'

So Milly-Molly-Mandy tied on an apron and became Jemima-Jane. And she washed up the breakfast things and put them away, and fetched whatever Mother wanted for cake-making from the larder and the cupboard, and picked over the sultanas (which was a nice job, as Jemima-Jane was allowed to eat as many sultanas as she had fingers on both hands, but not one more), and she beat the eggs in a basin, and stirred the cake-mixture in the bowl. And after Mother had filled the cake tins Jemima-Jane was allowed to put the scrapings into her own little patty-pan and bake it for her own self in the oven (and that sort of cake always tastes nicer than any other sort, only there's never enough of it!)

Well, it snowed and it snowed all day. Milly-Molly-Mandy kept running to the windows to look, but it didn't stop once. When Father and Grandpa and Uncle had to go out (to see after the cows and the pony and the chickens) they came back looking like snowmen.

'Is it good for sledging yet, Father?' asked Milly-Molly-Mandy.

'Getting better every minute, Milly-Molly-Mandy, that's certain,' answered Father, stamping snow off his boots on the door-mat.

'I wonder what Susan thinks of it, and if Billy

has nearly made his sledge yet,' said Milly-Molly-Mandy.

But it didn't stop snowing before dark, so she couldn't find out that day.

The next day, Sunday, the snow had stopped falling, and it looked beautiful, spread out all over everything. Father and Mother and Grandpa and Uncle and Aunty and Milly-Molly-Mandy put on their Wellington boots, or goloshes (Milly-Molly-Mandy had boots), and walked to Church. (Grandma didn't like walking in the snow, so she stayed at home to look after the fire and put the potatoes on.)

Billy Blunt was there with his father and mother, so afterwards in the lane Milly-Molly-Mandy asked him, 'Have you made your sledge yet?'

And Billy Blunt said, ''Tisn't finished. Dad's going to help me with it this afternoon. I'll be trying it out before school tomorrow, probably.'

Milly-Molly-Mandy was sorry it wasn't done yet. But anyhow she and little-friend-Susan had a grand time all that afternoon, making a snowman in the Moggs' front garden.

On Monday Milly-Molly-Mandy was in a great hurry to finish her breakfast and be off very early to school.

She didn't have long to wait for little-friend-Susan

either, and together they trudged along through the snow. It was quite hard going, for sometimes it was almost over the tops of their boots. (But they didn't always keep to the road!)

When they came to the Village there, just outside the corn-shop, was Billy Blunt's new sledge. And while they were looking at it Billy Blunt came out at the side gate.

'Hullo,' he said. 'Thought you weren't coming.'

'Hullo, Billy. Isn't that a beauty! Have you been on it yet? Can we have a ride?'

'You'll have to hurry, then,' said Billy Blunt, picking up the string. 'I've been up on the hill by Crocker's Farm, past the cross-roads.'

'I know,' said Milly-Molly-Mandy; 'near where that little girl Bunchy and her grandmother live. Can we go there now?'

'Hurry up, then,' said Billy Blunt.

So they all hurried up, through the Village, past the cross-roads and the school, along the road to Crocker's Hill, shuffling through the snow, dragging the sledge behind them.

'Isn't it deep here!' panted Milly-Molly-Mandy. 'This is the way Bunchy comes to school every day. I wonder how she'll manage today. She isn't very big.'

'We've come uphill a long way,' panted little-friend-Susan. 'Can't we sit on the sledge and go down now?'

'Oh, let's get to the top of the hill first,' panted Milly-Molly-Mandy.

'There's a steep bit there. You get a good run,' said Billy Blunt. 'I've done it six times. I went up before breakfast.'

'I wish I'd come too!' said Milly-Molly-Mandy.

'Sledge only holds one,' said Billy Blunt.

'Oh!' said Milly-Molly-Mandy.

'Oh!' said little-friend-Susan.

They hadn't thought of that.

'Which of us has first go?' said little-friend-Susan.

'Don't suppose there'll be time for more than one of you, anyhow,' said Billy Blunt. 'We've got to get back.'

'You have first go,' said Milly-Molly-Mandy to little-friend-Susan.

'No, you have first go,' said little-friend-Susan to Milly-Molly-Mandy.

'Better hurry,' said Billy Blunt. 'You'll be late for school.'

They struggled on up the last steep bit of the hill. And there were the little girl Bunchy and her

grandmother, hand-in-hand, struggling up it through the snow from the other side. The little cottage where they lived could be seen down below, with their two sets of footprints leading up from it.

'Hullo, Bunchy,' said Milly-Molly-Mandy.

'Oh! Hullo, Milly-Molly-Mandy,' said Bunchy. And Bunchy and her grandmother both looked very pleased to see them all. Grandmother had just been thinking she would have to take Bunchy all the way to school today.

But Milly-Molly-Mandy said, 'I'll take care of her.' And she took hold of Bunchy's little cold hand with her warm one (it was very warm indeed with pulling the sledge up the hill). 'You go down in the sledge, Susan, and I'll look after Bunchy.'

'No,' said little-friend-Susan. 'You wanted it just as much.'

'Sit *her* on it,' said Billy Blunt, pointing to Bunchy. 'We can run her to school in no time. Come on.'

So Bunchy had the ride, with Billy Blunt to guide the sledge and Milly-Molly-Mandy and little-friend-Susan to keep her safe on it. And Grandmother stood and watched them all go shouting down the steep bit. And then, as Bunchy was quite light and the road was a bit downhill most of the way, they pulled her along easily, right up to the school gate, in good time for school.

And Bunchy *did* enjoy her ride. She thought it was the excitingest thing that had ever happened!

And then after afternoon school (Bunchy had her dinner at school because it was too far for her to go home for it) Billy Blunt told her to get on his sledge again. And he and Milly-Molly-Mandy and little-friend-Susan pulled her all the way home (except up the steepest bit). And Grandmother was so grateful to them that she gave them each a warm currant bun.

And then Milly-Molly-Mandy and little-friend-Susan took turns riding down the hill on Billy Blunt's sledge. It went like the wind, so that you had to shriek like anything, and your cap blew off, and you felt you could go on for ever! And then, *Whoosh!* you landed sprawling in the snow just where the road turned near the bottom.

Milly-Molly-Mandy and little-friend-Susan each got tipped out there. But when Billy Blunt had gone to the top of the hill with the sledge for his turn he came sailing down and rounded the bend like a bird, and went on and on and was almost at the cross-roads when the others caught him up. (But then, he'd had plenty of practice, and nobody had seen him spill out at his first try!)

It seemed a long walk home to the nice white cottage with the thatched roof after all that, and Milly-Molly-Mandy was quite late for tea. But Father and Mother and Grandpa and Grandma and

Uncle and Aunty weren't a bit cross, because they guessed what she had been up to, and of course, you can't go sledging every day!

In fact, it rained that very night, and next day the snow was nearly all gone. So wasn't it a good thing that Billy Blunt had got his sledge made in time?